To my sisters, who showed me how to move big mountains – F.S.

A TEMPLAR BOOK

First Published in Switzerland in 2018 as *Geh weg, Herr Berg!* by Atlantis, an imprint of Orell Füssli Verlag,
Sicherheitsdruc AG, Zurich, Switzerland.

This edition first published in the UK in 2021 by Templar Books, an imprint of Bonnier Books UK,
The Plaza, 535 King's Road, London, SW10 0SZ
Owned by Bonnier Books
Sveavägen 56, Stockholm, Sweden
www.templarco.co.uk • www.bonnierbooks.co.uk

1 3 5 7 9 10 8 6 4 2

MIX
Paper from
responsible sources
FSC
www.fsc.org
FSC® C104723

English edition edited by Joanna McInerney and Samuel Fern
Additional design by Olivia Cook
Production by Nick Read

ISBN: 978-1-78741-805-9

This book was typeset in Melloner Happy and Mrs Ant
The illustrations were created digitally

Printed in China

MOVE, MR MOUNTAIN!

Francesca Sanna

Mr Mountain had seen a lot in his lifetime.
He didn't mind when the humans climbed up his shoulders or skiied
down his hips, and he didn't mind when they played him songs
on their strange instruments. In fact, he liked that most of all.

A long life lay ahead of Mr Mountain, and he was determined to spend
it resting. Because he had seen it all, nothing could ever disturb him . . .
or at least that is what he thought.

One day, Mr Mountain heard a sharp voice shouting at him. Who dared to disturb his rest? He looked down, to find a young girl staring at him angrily.

"I said, CAN YOU MOVE, PLEASE?"

The mountain was shocked, but he was determined not to lose his temper. He was a mountain after all. He inhaled the fresh air around his top, breathed in and counted to ten.

Then, he calmly answered, "Young lady, I think you misunderstand. I am the great Mr Mountain! **Nobody** asks me to move, and certainly, if someone were to ask me to move, they would do it more *politely*."

"I am Lily," answered the little girl. "And I meant what I said. You see, the window of my room faces your rocky sides. Every morning I wake up with the same view. If you move, I can finally see what is behind you."

Mr Mountain was confused. "I cannot move. You have legs, you can climb
over me. There is no need to disturb a big mountain with your little problems."

Lily was furious. "I want to see what's behind you!" she shouted.
"I cannot climb and even if I could, it would take me a very long time.
I need you to move . . . **NOW!**"

Enough was enough. The age-old patience of the mountain vanished.
As quick as a flash, Mr Mountain collected the clouds around his head . . .

. . . and squeezed them hard. Endless, thundering rain
began to pour down on the tiny houses in the village,
and huge puddles began to form on the ground.

Lily pulled on her raincoat and ran outside. She danced in the puddles
and tried to catch the falling raindrops in her mouth. "Thank you for this rain,
Mr Mountain. It is very refreshing. But can you **please** move now?"

Mr Mountain was beginning to lose his temper.
He inhaled all the air he possibly could, and then blew
it out across the land as a strong, freezing wind.

Every tree bent in the storm. But Lily was having too much fun.
"I like this breeze, Mr Mountain. How very nice of you!" she teased.
"But can you move out of the way now, please?"

Mr Mountain was tired, but willing to try anything
to stop this little human. He reached for the snow on
his shoulders, and sprinkled it all over the village.

Lily was euphoric. "SNOW!" she cried.
"This is getting better and better. Thank you, Mr Mountain!
But, back to my request, could you move already?"

Mr Mountain was exhausted. What else could he try? This small girl was not going to change her mind. "*Please?*" she insisted. Then he had an idea. He reached out his rocky hand, and scooped Lily up from the ground.

"What are you doing?" she asked.

"You will see," he answered. Carefully, Mr Mountain stretched his arm up and put Lily down on the top of his head. "Here you are. Are you happy now?" he groaned.

Lily blinked . . .

. . . and then, she saw it – the other side of the mountain.
She saw every tree and every hill, every city and every house,
and behind that, the sea! It was better than anything she
could have imagined. **"How wonderful!"** she gasped.

Lily sat on Mr Mountain's peak for hours.
Together, they invented names for the cities they could
see in the distance, and for the streets and hills behind them.
They imagined what it might be like to live there,
and dreamed of visiting all those places.

The next day, Lily decided she was going to learn how to climb.
Little by little, and with some help from Mr Mountain, she could soon
reach the very top all by herself. Mr Mountain was very proud,
and strangely happy to finally have a friend to spend his time with.

But one day, Lily didn't visit. At first he thought she was busy, but the days soon turned into weeks, and then months. Mr Mountain became sad. This was a very strange feeling for an old mountain who hadn't had much company in millions of years. He missed having Lily around.

Mr Mountain grew sadder and sadder.

He missed Lily so much that his tears rained all over the village.
His body **shook** and **shivered** and the earth
around him **trembled** and **rumbled**.

The villagers grew sad too. They strengthened their homes
and never went outside without an umbrella.
Months passed by and still Mr Mountain was glum.

One morning, Mr Mountain awoke to a day like any other,
with grey clouds swirling around his face. But suddenly
he heard a familiar voice, calling through the mist:

"Hello, Mr Mountain!"

And then she appeared! She was a little taller, but with the same
heartwarming smile. This was no ordinary day at all – Lily was back!

How Mr Mountain would have loved to jump in the air with joy!

Lily had **so many** stories to tell him. Stories about her travels around the world, and the people she had met. She showed him pictures of the countries she had visited – and even the other mountains she had climbed!

Mr Mountain could not move, but with Lily's photos, he could finally see the rest of the world.

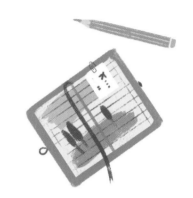

Now, every time Lily comes back from her travels, she visits
Mr Mountain with a new story to tell, and a new photograph to show him.
And each time she does this, the weather in the village is always sunny.